EMMA
Every Day

Crazy for Apples

by C.L. Reid

illustrated by Elena Aiello

PICTURE WINDOW BOOKS
a capstone imprint

Emma Every Day is published by
Picture Window Books, an imprint of Capstone
1710 Roe Crest Drive, North Mankato, Minnesota 56003
www.capstonepub.com

Library of Congress Cataloging-in-Publication Data
Names: Reid, C.L., author. | Aiello, Elena (Illustrator), illustrator.
Title: Crazy for apples / by C.L. Reid ; illustrated by Elena Aiello.
Description: North Mankato, Minnesota : Picture Window Books, a
Capstone imprint, 2020. | Series: Emma every day | Audience: Ages 5-7.

Summary: Emma, a Deaf girl, and her best friend, Izzie, are going to
the apple orchard today in order to pick apples for cooking, but their
basket of apples ends up in the mud. Includes an ASL fingerspelling
chart, glossary, and content-related questions.

Identifiers: LCCN 2020001364 (print) | LCCN 2020001365 (ebook) |
ISBN 9781515871828 (hardcover) | ISBN 9781515873136 (paperback) |
ISBN 9781515871903 (adobe pdf)

Subjects: LCSH: Deaf children—Juvenile fiction. | Apples—Harvesting—
Juvenile fiction. | Orchards—Juvenile fiction. | Best friends—Juvenile
fiction. | CYAC: Deaf—Fiction. | People with disabilities—Fiction.
| Apples—Fiction. | Orchards—Fiction. | Best friends—Fiction. |
Friendship—Fiction.

Classification: LCC PZ7.1.R4544 Cr 2020 (print) |
LCC PZ7.1.R4544 (ebook) | DDC [E]—dc23
LC record available at https://lccn.loc.gov/2020001364
LC ebook record available at https://lccn.loc.gov/2020001365

Image Credits: Capstone: Daniel Griffo, 28, 29 top left, Margeaux
Lucas, 29 bottom right, Randy Chewning, 29 top right, 29 bottom left
Design Elements: Shutterstock: achii, Mari C, Mika Besfamilnaya

Designer: Tracy McCabe

Printed and bound in the United States
PA117

TABLE OF CONTENTS

MEET EMMA

EMMA CARTER
Age: 8 Grade: 3

SIBLING

One brother, Jaden
(12 years old)

PARENTS
David and Lucy

BEST FRIEND
Izzie Jackson

PET
a goldfish named Ruby

favorite color: **teal**
favorite food: **tacos**
favorite school subject: **writing**
favorite sport: **swimming**
hobbies: **reading, writing, biking, swimming**

FINGERSPELLING GUIDE

MANUAL ALPHABET

Aa   Bb   Cc   Dd   Ee

Ff   Gg   Hh   Ii   Jj

MANUAL NUMBERS

0   1   2   3

Emma is Deaf. She uses American Sign Language (ASL) to communicate with her family. She also uses a Cochlear Implant (CI) to help her hear.

Kk Ll Mm Nn Oo

Pp Qq Rr Ss Tt Uu

Vv Ww Xx Yy Zz

4 5 6 7 8 9 10

Chapter 1

Apple Day

Emma was so excited! Today her dad was taking her to the apple orchard.

Emma was bringing her best friend, Izzie.

"Are you girls ready?" Emma's dad signed.

"I am," Izzie signed.

Emma put on her Cochlear Implant (CI). Then she grabbed her rain boots and coat.

"Me too! Let's go!" Emma said.

As soon as they got to the orchard, it started raining. Farmer Bell drove up in a tractor pulling a trailer filled with hay.

"I'm glad I wore my rain boots," Izzie signed.

"Same here!" Emma signed back.

"Are you girls ready?" Farmer Bell signed.

"You know ASL?" Emma signed.

"I do. My daughter is Deaf. She works here too," he signed.

Emma and Izzie climbed onto the trailer.  An empty basket sat between them. They had to wait while Emma's dad got his basket.

Muddy puddles covered the road.
The trailer bumped along.

"Dad, can we help you make apple treats when we get home?" Emma asked.

"Sure! What kind do you want to make?" Dad asked.

"Apple tarts," Izzie said.

"And apple pies, applesauce, and apple dumplings," Emma said.

With a final jolt, the trailer stopped. Farmer Bell helped everyone off the trailer.

"Have fun!" he signed, smiling.

Chapter 2
Apple Attack

"Let's go pick some yummy apples," Izzie said.

She grabbed their basket and started down the path. Emma followed.

The girls picked apples from the lower branches. They picked as many as they could. Emma's dad picked from the higher branches.

"Choose the crunchiest," he said. "They're better for baking."

Bonk!

"Ouch!  What was that?" Emma said, rubbing the top of her head.

"You were attacked by an apple," Izzie said, pointing to one on the ground.

Emma made a face and laughed.

Then she grabbed the apple off the

ground. She plopped it into their

basket, which was now full.

Emma and Izzie lugged the
basket back to the road. They
plopped onto a bench to wait for
Farmer Bell. But the bench was wet.
Emma slipped right off.

"What a day!" Emma said, laughing.

"At least we still have our apples," Izzie said.

"And lots of them," Emma's dad said.

Minutes later the tractor pulling the trailer rumbled up and stopped. Farmer Bell was back!

The girls put their basket on the trailer and climbed in.

"Hold on!" Farmer Bell called out to the group.

The tractor jerked forward. The trailer bounced along behind. It hit a big rut, and the girls' basket tipped right off the trailer!

Splash!

All the apples rolled into a muddy puddle!

Chapter 3
Candy

The trailer slowed and halted.

Farmer Bell checked the fallen

apples.

"These aren't good anymore,"

he said. "Sorry, girls."

"It's okay. I still have my apples," Emma's dad said.

"Don't worry. I'll get Candy when we get back to the store," Farmer Bell said.

"Candy? Is he going to give us candy?" Emma signed to Izzie.

"I don't know," Izzie signed. "But I do like candy."

Ten minutes later, they pulled up in front of Bell's Apple Store. Farmer Bell hurried inside.

Emma's dad, Emma, and Izzie wandered into the store. A young woman carrying a big bag  of apples met them.

"Hello, I'm Candy Bell," she
signed as she handed the bag to
Emma. "My dad said you lost
your apples."

"Thank you," Emma signed.
She noticed Candy had a CI.

"I use a CI too!" Emma signed.

Candy smiled. "I love my CI,

but I still sign most of the time."

"Me too," Emma signed.

"And Emma taught me

ASL,"  Izzie signed.

"That's great!" Candy signed.

Then Farmer Bell came over with Emma's dad. They had a tray of apple treats.

"Dig in," Farmer Bell said.

It was the perfect end to a crazy, rainy apple orchard day.

LEARN TO SIGN

good
Move hand away from mouth.

sad
Move hands down in front of face.

rain
Move hands down.

autumn
Move hand past elbow twice, like a leaf falling from a tree.

candy

Twist finger on cheek.

cook

Move hand back and forth.

tree

Wiggle wrist back forth.

apple

Wiggle X shape at corner of mouth.

GLOSSARY

Cochlear Implant (also called CI)—a device that helps someone who is Deaf to hear; it is worn on the head just above the ear

communicate—to pass along thoughts, feelings, or information

deaf—being unable to hear

fingerspell—to make letters with your hands to spell out words; often used for names of people and places

halted—stopped

lugged—carried something with lots of effort

rut—a deep, narrow track in the ground made by wheels

sign—use hand gestures to communicate

sign language—a language in which hand gestures, along with facial expressions and body movements, are used instead of speech

TALK ABOUT IT

1. Emma's favorite season is fall. Talk about your favorite season.

2. A lot of things went wrong for Emma in the story. Do you think she still had a fun day? Why or why not?

3. Were you surprised by the ending of the story? Why or why not?

WRITE ABOUT IT

1. Make a list of at least five activities you like to do during your favorite season.

2. Emma's best friend is Izzie. Write a paragraph about your best friend.

3. There were a few clues in the story leading up to the apples falling off the trailer and into the mud. Look back and make a list of at least three of those clues.

ABOUT THE AUTHOR

Deaf-blind since childhood, C.L. Reid received a Cochlear Implant (CI) as an adult to help her hear, and she uses American Sign Language (ASL) to communicate. She and her husband have three sons. Their middle son is also deaf-blind. Reid earned a master's degree in writing for children and young adults at Hamline University in St. Paul, Minnesota. Reid lives in Minnesota with her husband, two of their sons, and their cats.

ABOUT THE ILLUSTRATOR

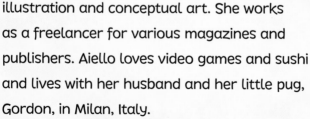

Elena Aiello is an illustrator and character designer. After graduating as a marketing specialist, she decided to study art direction and CGI. Doing so, she discovered a passion for illustration and conceptual art. She works as a freelancer for various magazines and publishers. Aiello loves video games and sushi and lives with her husband and her little pug, Gordon, in Milan, Italy.